NEXT IN LINE

SUDDENLY
ROYAL

NEXT IN
LINE

VANESSA ACTON

Darby Creek
A division of Lerner Publishing Group, Inc.
241 First Avenue North
Minneapolis, MN 55401 USA

For reading levels and more information, look up this title at www.lernerbooks.com.

Cover and interior images: Igor Klimov/Shutterstock.com (background texture); GoMixer/Shutterstock.com (coat of arms and lion); KazanovskyAndrey/iStock/Getty Images Plus (gold); mona redshinestudio/Shutterstock.com (crown).

Main body text set in Janson Text LT Std 12/17.5.
Typeface provided by Adobe Systems.

Library of Congress Cataloging-in-Publication Data

Names: Acton, Vanessa, author.
Title: Next in line / by Vanessa Acton.
Description: Minneapolis : Darby Creek, [2018] I Series: Suddenly royal I Summary:
   A high school junior in suburban Ohio learns that she is actually next in line to the
   throne of the kingdom of Evonia.
Identifiers: LCCN 2017044419 (print) I LCCN 2017056236 (ebook) I
   ISBN 9781541525955 (eb pdf) I ISBN 9781541525719 (lb : alk. paper) I
   ISBN 9781541526389 (pb : alk. paper)
Subjects: I CYAC: Princesses—Fiction.
Classification: LCC PZ7.1.A228 (ebook) I LCC PZ7.1.A228 Ne 2018 (print) I DDC
   [Fic]—dc23

LC record available at https://lccn.loc.gov/2017044419

Manufactured in the United States of America
1-44555-35486-1/30/2018

For K.P., the best bodyguard
a story could have

The Valmont Family of Evonia

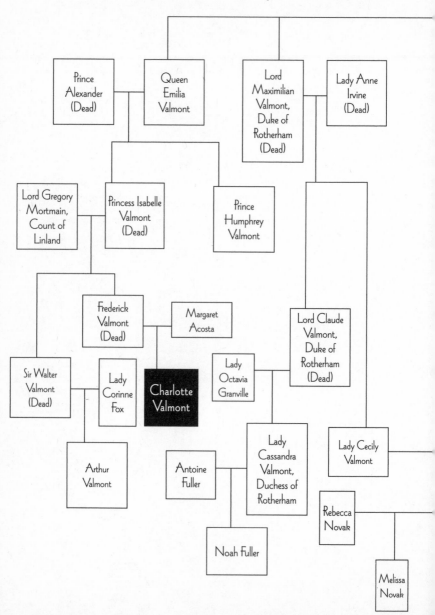

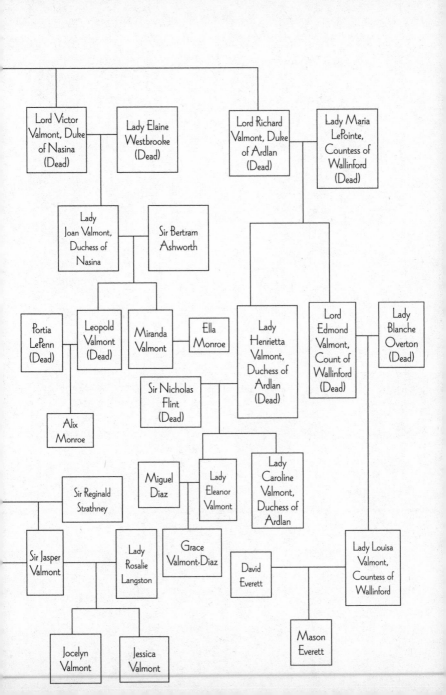

1

"Wait—I'm a *what*?"

Carly Valmont stared at her mom, who sat across from her at the scratched-up kitchen table.

Her mom gave her an embarrassed smile. "Your full title is Princess Royal of the Kingdom of Evonia."

"Princess," Carly echoed numbly. This was not at all what she'd expected when she'd sat down with her mom and stepdad to talk about college applications.

"And second in line for the throne," her mom added timidly. "After Queen Emilia, your great-grandmother, dies, your great-uncle, Crown Prince Humphrey, will become king.

He has no children, so you're technically his heir."

Carly had never even heard of these people. Of course she'd heard of Evonia, the tiny European country where her dad had been born. But she didn't even remember her dad, thanks to the heart attack that had killed him when she was barely a year old. Who were these random royal relatives of his? And how could *she*, a regular high school junior in suburban Ohio, be a *princess*?

"That's . . . insane," said Carly. Normally, she was better at choosing her words before she spoke. She hadn't become captain of her school's debate team by accident. But this news was such a curveball that she knew it was pointless to try coming up with a more measured response. "Why didn't you ever tell me this before?"

Her mom shot a glance at Sal, Carly's stepdad, who stood off to the side, leaning on the kitchen counter. Sal seemed to be very absorbed in picking dirt out from under his nails. Seeing that he would be no help, Carly's mom said, "Evonia is your dad's country, not mine. And since you never got a chance to know your dad, and our life has always been here, I . . . didn't want to burden you with all this until you were old enough to handle it."

Carly took a deep breath and looked down at the college mailers she'd collected over the past several months. Just ten minutes ago, she'd been thinking about which schools she'd like to visit this summer, which ones had the best pre-law programs, which ones gave the best scholarships to top students like her. Her mom and Sal were always telling her to aim high, so it had puzzled her that they'd been so reluctant to talk about her college plans. She'd assumed it was because tuition was so expensive. Not because they'd known she could aim way higher than an advanced degree.

"I'm sorry to dump everything on you all at once, honey," her mom continued in a rush. "But your grandfather's been asking me to bring you over there this summer—"

"Grandpa G?" Her dad's father. The only member of her dad's family she'd ever had any contact with. A clipped, British-sounding accent over the phone on her birthday. A cheerfully dignified email at the holidays—always addressing her by her full name, Charlotte. Really nice presents that she'd always appreciated. But otherwise a stranger.

"Yeah," her mom confirmed. "Grandpa G is Lord Gregory Mortmain, the Count of Linland."

"Lord, not prince?" She wasn't sure why she was zeroing in on titles, except that it was the most concrete thing she could grasp right now.

"That's right. He's not a prince because he wasn't born into the royal family. He married into it."

"Like you did," guessed Carly. "When you married my dad."

Her mom gave an awkward little shrug. "Yeah."

"So what's *your* title?" Carly asked her a little accusingly.

Looking over at Sal again, Carly's mom said, "I don't have a title anymore. While I was married to your dad I was technically Lady Margaret Valmont, but now I'm just plain Maggie Acosta."

Carly turned to Sal. "Did you know about this all along?"

"Uh, well." Sal shrugged sheepishly. "It came up at some point when I was dating your mom."

So basically, yes, he had known about it all along. Sal had married Carly's mom when Carly was four. He was the only dad she remembered. And he'd kept this secret from her too.

"So you're telling me I'm going to, like, rule an entire country someday."

"Well, Evonia's a constitutional monarchy," her mom explained quickly. "The royal family doesn't have any real power. The government's run by elected officials—a parliament. The queen's duties are just ceremonial. It's the same for the royal family in England."

Carly's brain was slowly starting to wrap around what this meant.

"Honey, listen," said her mom, sounding almost desperately apologetic. "I know this is a shock. And I wish we'd figured out a better way to explain everything to you earlier . . ."

"I wish you had too," said Carly. "If I'd known, I wouldn't have been so worried about college! It's not like I need to pick a career path if I'm going to be a queen, right?"

"Um, that's a fair point," her mom said, looking a little surprised.

"And I won't have to worry about money, I'm guessing?"

"Nooo," said her mom cautiously, drawing out the word. "The royal family is supported by taxes that the Evonian citizens pay."

Carly nodded in satisfaction. "Just like US politicians get their salaries from tax money that the government collects."

"Right, I guess," said Carly's mom. "I never spent much time in Evonia, but from what I remember, your dad's family lives pretty comfortably."

Huge knots of tension in Carly's shoulder and back muscles dissolved instantly. All year she'd been stressing about how her family could afford sending her to college, about what career path she should choose. Her teachers said she'd make a great lawyer, a great politician, a great CEO, a great this, a great that. High-intensity jobs, every single one of them. Jobs with long hours and huge stakes and miles of loans to pay off. Now it turned out she could be a *queen* someday instead.

Queen of her dad's country. Following in her dad's footsteps. She couldn't count how many times her mom had said to her "We're so proud of you—and your dad would be so proud too." After every good report card, every school choir concert and debate competition. It had always felt a little tacked on, a little forced. But becoming a queen: *that* definitely would've made her dad proud.

"We thought you'd be a little more freaked out about it," said Sal.

Carly laughed. "This is actually a gigantic relief! I've been assuming that the rest of my life depends on where I go to college, what major I pick. Now the pressure's off!"

Sal grinned at her, and her mom let out a long breath. "Well," her mom said, "you might have to do *some* planning. At least when it comes to how you'll spend your summer. Your grandfather has offered to pay for you to fly out to Evonia for a couple of months after school lets out. You can meet your other Evonian relatives, see the sights, get a sense of the country's culture . . ."

Carly could barely believe that minutes earlier, she'd expected to spend her summer listening to boring campus tour guides and trying to impress college admissions staff. "That sounds amazing," she told her mom. "When do I leave?"

2

The night before Carly flew to Evonia, the whole family went out for ice cream. Sal had suggested dinner, but no one could agree on a restaurant. When it came to ice cream, there was never a debate.

"Bet they don't have Frozen Paradise in Evonia," said Carly's thirteen-year-old half-brother Nic as the five of them sat down at a table.

"No, but there's a famous ice cream shop in Alaborn, the capital city. I read about it on some tourism sites. It's more than *two hundred* years old."

"Can't be as good as Frozen Paradise," Nic said firmly.

"When she's queen she can build a hundred Frozen Paradises there if she wants to," said Rafe, Carly's other half-brother.

Nic slurped around the edge of his cone. "Pretty sure Mom told us that Carly will have zero power. If she wants decent ice cream she'll have to ask the senate or whatever."

"Parliament," said Carly through a mouthful of chocolate fudge. Over the past few weeks, she'd made a point of getting her Evonian-related facts straight. She could rattle off the basics from memory: The Evonian monarchy stretched back to the fourteenth century. The royals had given up their governing powers fifty years ago. Now the kingdom was a constitutional monarchy, which was where the parliament came in. "But if I really need the best ice cream in the world I'll just come back here."

"Oh, I see how it is," teased Sal. "I kinda thought you'd want to come back and see your family, but it's all about the food. Good to know where we stand."

"I'd definitely come back for *your* food," Carly told him with a grin. "As long as you only made my favorites. You can't order a future queen to eat broccoli."

"Hey, will you be able to drive here without a license?" Nic cut in. "And be exempt from speeding tickets and stuff? Diplomatic immunity, right, like people get in movies?"

"Whoa," said Rafe. "Carly, if you can't get arrested in the States there's some stuff I need you to do for me."

"It'd be my pleasure, sir," said Carly. "Just waiting on the bribe."

"If I bribe a member of a foreign royal family is that treason?"

"Nah," said Sal. "It's just a felony."

It felt cheesy to be hanging out with her whole family like this on her last night, but she was enjoying it. And she wouldn't see them again for two months. Her grandfather had offered to buy them all plane tickets to Evonia, but her parents couldn't get time off work, and the boys were already signed up for summer camp.

Carly had never flown across the ocean before. Had never been away from her family for so long. But she didn't feel any nervousness, just a fizzing excitement in her veins.

She was ready. She still had her passport from when the family had taken a trip to the Canadian side of Niagara Falls a few years ago. She'd revised her packing list a dozen times. Bought little converters for all her power cords so that they'd fit in Europe's weirdly-shaped outlets. Gotten some of her allowance money converted to euros. Downloaded a messaging app on her phone so that she could keep in touch with her family while she was gone. Read and reread her grandfather's email about the travel arrangements. And spent hours researching Evonia online.

She'd kept expecting her mom to offer to help, to give her advice, or just to tell her more about this country. But her mom had been weirdly quiet.

Even now, as everyone else joked around, Carly's mom just stared thoughtfully at the ridges of her waffle cone.

"You okay, Mom?" Carly asked.

Her mom snapped out of it and smiled at her. "I'm fine, honey. But we'd better wrap this up and head home soon."

"Mom, it's Friday!" Rafe protested. "Live on the edge."

"Your sister has a very a long day tomorrow. She'll need a good night's sleep beforehand."

Carly wanted to ask what was bothering her mom, but she didn't want to spoil the warm, comfortable feeling of her family being together. *Maybe she's just thinking about how much she'll miss me while I'm gone. And how fast I'm growing up. All the usual stuff parents get mopey about.*

But she couldn't escape the feeling that something else was up. Her mom didn't seem to be *happy* for her, which didn't make any sense. She was always saying, "We want you to live the best possible life." Well, mission accomplished—or soon to be accomplished. Her mom should be thrilled.

Sal caught her eye, then typed something into his phone. A moment later Carly's phone buzzed. They sometimes played this game—texting each other when they didn't want Carly's mom to know what they were saying.

The text from Sal said *Don't worry about her. She's gonna be fine. Just enjoy this opportunity!*

Carly smiled and texted back, *Deal.*

***

The flight to Europe was nine hours long. Carly entertained herself by watching movies and ordering far too many snacks. She'd never flown first-class before and was amazed at all the options. Not to mention the extra leg room. *Thanks for the upgrade, Grandpa G,* she thought. *If this is what it's like to be royalty, I am so in.*

She also flipped through the guidebook her grandfather had sent her. It had shown up in the mail just yesterday, so she hadn't had time to look at it yet.

Mostly it contained the same basic information about Evonia that she'd already found online.

A tiny, often-forgotten country a quarter of the size of Rhode Island . . .

*Rich cultural landscape that draws from its
neighbors, France and Germany, as well as later
English and Dutch influences . . .*

*Attracts enough tourists to outnumber
its residents . . .*

A hidden treasure seemingly outside of time.

That kind of stuff. But it was cool to look
at the photos of breathtaking scenery and
centuries-old buildings. It was cool—and still
fairly mind-boggling—to think, *This is my
country. Someday I'm going to be the queen of
this country.*

Sipping her third complimentary soda of
the flight, she could hardly wait.

3

Evonia was too small to have its own airport. The plane touched down in France. Carly's grandfather had warned her about this in his email. He'd told her that he'd send someone to meet her and take her to his private plane for the last leg of the journey.

As Carly stepped off the plane, a burly middle-aged guy dressed like he belonged in the Secret Service approached her. "Charlotte Valmont?" he asked in a low voice.

"Yes?"

"Your grandfather sent me." His accent was similar to Carly's grandfather's—not quite British, but not quite anything else she could put her finger on. He reached for her rolling suitcase. "Allow me, your highness . . ."

Your highness. It sounded so weird, so unreal. "Um, that's okay," said Carly. "It's not that heavy. And I mean, it's got wheels. I'm good."

"Very well. We'll collect the rest of your luggage before we—"

"I didn't bring any other luggage," Carly said. "Just this."

The man paused. His expression was blank, but Carly could tell his brain was taking some time to process this information. Then he said, "Very well. Come with me then."

He started walking, but Carly hung back. "How do I know you're not kidnapping me?" she said half-jokingly.

The guy turned and blinked once in slow motion. It was unnerving.

Carly tried again. "I mean, how do I know you're really who my grandfather sent? Instead of some random person just pretending to work for him?"

"Ah," he said in a weary voice. "I was

warned that Americans watch a great deal of television." With a sigh, he pulled out a phone, dialed a number, and spoke into it. "My lord? Your granddaughter is here with me. She requests confirmation of my identity. Yes, my lord."

He handed Carly the phone.

"Charlotte?" said the familiar voice on the other end.

"Um, hi," Carly said. "Just checking that I wasn't about to get snatched and held for ransom."

"Wise girl," said her grandfather in an approving tone. "That would be inconvenient for all of us. I believe you can trust Seton. I run very thorough background checks on all my staff."

"Good to know. I guess I'll see you soon then."

"Safe travels," he said briskly before ending the call.

Feeling slightly awkward, Carly handed the phone back to the Secret Service guy. "Guess you're legit, Seton. Lead the way."

"With pleasure," Seton replied in a voice that would've been sarcastic if it hadn't been so clipped.

***

From the window of her grandfather's little plane, Carly watched the landscape glide by below her. It was late morning here, so she could see everything clearly. The land was green and mountainous and beautiful, but it also looked shockingly empty. Other than the occasional light dot that looked like a distant farmhouse and one narrow winding line of a road, the place looked untouched. *Seemingly outside of time*, as the guidebook had said.

After about twenty minutes, something caught Carly's eye. A house—a palace?—some kind of massive building. As the plane circled closer, Carly could see ramparts on the roof, turrets sticking up at the corners, pretty much everything except a drawbridge.

"Mortmain Castle," said Seton, who sat across from her. "The family home of the Count of Linland."

"Isn't it kind of overkill that he's a lord *and* a count?" Carly asked. All the different names and titles still confused her. She still hadn't figured out why her dad had ended up with his mother's surname, Valmont, instead of his father's, Mortmain.

Seton remained expressionless. "Some might call it overkill to bother dividing such a small country into even smaller provinces. But here we are, at the mercy of our ancestors' questionable decisions."

Carly wasn't totally sure what he meant by that. But it sounded unpleasant.

Mortmain Castle, on the other hand, looked gorgeous. Carly felt her excitement bubbling up again as she looked at it. *Hello, province of Linland*, she thought. *Hello, kingdom of Evonia. I'm your future queen.*

4

The plane landed on a little private airstrip within spitting distance of the castle. Nearby, a very tall, stick-thin, white-haired man waited next to a sleek black car. He was dressed in crisp khaki pants and a sweater that looked too warm for the weather. Carly suddenly felt very conscious of her rumpled jeans and T-shirt.

"So, not kidnapped, I presume?" he called out as Carly and Seton walked over to him.

"I guess not," Carly said, smiling.

Her grandfather glanced at Seton.

"Seton, why is the girl carrying her own suitcase?"

"She insisted, my lord," said Seton. "And she claimed she brought no other luggage with her."

"Well!" said Carly's grandfather, clearly impressed. "I've always admired people who know how to pack light. Arthur could learn a thing or two from her."

"Who's Arthur?" Carly asked, standing awkwardly next to her grandfather. She'd been expecting some kind of welcoming hug or at least a kiss on the cheek, but the window for that sort of gesture seemed to have closed.

Her grandfather sighed. "Arthur is your cousin. The son of your father's brother. Here—let me introduce you."

He opened the passenger door of the car and leaned in. "Arthur, kindly step out of the car and greet Charlotte."

Carly peered over her grandfather's shoulder. Inside the car, a guy around her age sat slumped against the plush seats. He was holding a phone and wearing headphones studded with what looked like actual diamonds. Carly knew headphones like that *existed*, but she'd never known anyone who could afford them. Other than that, this guy looked fairly ordinary. He was wearing jeans and a T-shirt.

The shirt said *Life is pain, get over it*. A bit of a mismatch with the diamond-studded headphones, in Carly's opinion.

"Arthur," her grandfather said more loudly. "If you could do us the courtesy of making eye contact for a moment . . ."

Arthur glanced up from his phone. "Sorry, m'lord, did you say something?" he said with a faint sneer.

Off to the side, Seton coughed into his sleeve. The cough sounded suspiciously like "Pointless."

Carly's grandfather sighed. "Charlotte, this Arthur. Why don't you climb in? You can sit next to him during the ride to the castle."

Carly shot a confused glance at the impressive stone structure a few hundred yards from them. "Isn't the castle, like, right there? Within walking distance?"

"Walking distance!" her grandfather laughed. "She's delightful, isn't she, Seton? Go on, my dear, get in the car."

So Carly got in. She sat in the middle, with Arthur slouched on one side of her and her grandfather sitting primly on her other side. Seton put her luggage in the trunk and then climbed into the front passenger seat. The driver—Carly hadn't noticed him before— drove the car up a wide, tree-lined pathway and through an elaborate iron gate.

Fifty-three seconds later, they got back out of the car.

"Welcome to my humble cottage," said Carly's grandfather. "It's nothing compared to the royal palace in Alaborn. But I find it quite comfortable."

"It's beautiful," Carly said, craning to look up at the towers.

"We only live in one wing," said Arthur in a bored voice. He still hadn't removed the headphones or put away his phone. "The rest of the place is a nightmare. Completely falling apart. When I inherit it I'll have to spend a fortune making it decent."

"So good to see you thinking ahead, Arthur," said their grandfather dryly.

By this time, Seton had retrieved Carly's suitcase from the trunk of the car. Carly's grandfather looked over at him. "Bring that up to the princess's rooms, Seton. And then escort her to luncheon at noon." He looked back at Carly. "We'll give you a couple of hours to refresh yourself."

Just the thought of having some down time made Carly realize how tired she was. Her first flight had left the United States early Saturday evening, and she hadn't slept since. If it was ten in the morning here, it was the middle of the night back home. Smothering a yawn, she said, "Thanks, Grandpa."

"*Grandpa?*" echoed Arthur mockingly. "You're supposed to call him *my lord*. Isn't she, m'lord?"

Their grandfather pursed his lips. "Technically, yes—"

"And shouldn't the girl who's second-in-line for the throne show proper respect for our ancient customs and titles?"

"You're hardly one to talk, Arthur," said their grandfather.

"I'm just saying, if she can't handle something as simple as that—"

"I think I've got it now, thanks," Carly cut in, hoping her tone came across as firm but polite, instead of furious. She turned to her grandfather. "Sorry about the confusion, m'lord," she said, running the words together the same way Arthur did.

I'll think of him as Lord G, she decided. *Lord Gregory—Lord Grandfather. It's at least half human.*

"Not to worry, my dear. We'll see you at luncheon. Dress code is business casual."

Seriously? A dress code, for lunch? Carly wanted to ask if Arthur would be changing into old-man pants and a tasteful sweater. But Lord G was clearly done with the conversation. He started walking around the side of the house. Arthur frowned down at his phone, ignoring Carly again.

Carly followed Seton—and her suitcase—through the imposing front doors.

The front hall practically swallowed her up. Carly had never seen such a high ceiling except in a museum. Portraits in elaborate gold frames lined the walls on either side of a huge stone staircase. Carly stared at the imposing figures in the portraits as she hurried after Seton. Some of these paintings had to be hundreds of years old, judging by the clothes the people were wearing. Everyone looked stiff and grim, as if they'd just heard unpleasant news.

Especially the woman in the portrait at the top of the stairs. She seemed to be eyeing Carly and thinking *Who's this random kid?*

Seton was already climbing the staircase. "Your rooms are on the second floor, your highness," he said over his shoulder.

Carly followed him up the steps, gripping the smooth marble banister. "So, uh, what's my cousin Arthur's deal? Does he live here with our grandfather?"

"He does now. His father, your uncle Walter, died six years ago, as I'm sure you know." She vaguely remembered this. Her mom had sent a condolence card to her grandfather. But it hadn't really been on Carly's radar. She felt a surge of sympathy for her cousin—along with a twinge of guilt that she'd never asked about this uncle.

"A few years after that," Seton went on, "Arthur came to stay here. His mother, Lady Corinne, found Arthur to be—to use her own words—too much work."

Carly winced. "Eesh. That's a pretty cold thing to say about your own kid." It was hard to imagine either of her parents wanting to pawn off any of their children on someone else.

"I do not comment on family matters," Seton replied neutrally. "I merely work here."

At the top of the staircase, Seton headed down a long hallway. After passing several doors, he finally stopped in front of one and set Carly's suitcase down. "Your sitting room, bedroom, and bathroom are in there, your highness. I'll let you settle in for the next few hours. If you need anything, you can call the housekeeper from the phone in your bedroom. I'll be out here in the meantime. I'll knock on your door a few minutes before noon and take you down to luncheon."

Carly stood with one hand on her suitcase and one hand on the doorknob. This whole setup felt incredibly uncomfortable. "You really don't have to lead me around the whole time I'm here, Seton. I mean, it's nice of you to show me where everything is, but I'll figure it out. You can—you know—leave me to my own devices."

"I'm afraid I can't, your highness," said Seton. "As your bodyguard, I have a duty to—"

"Wait, did you say bodyguard?"

"I did."

"Oh." Why hadn't she expected this? The US president's family had a whole department of bodyguards. Everyone that important had security personnel. Carly just hadn't realized she was that important. "Guess that's why the kidnapping joke didn't land very well?"

"Right," said Seton.

And you have no sense of humor, Carly thought.

"I'll wait out here until it's time for luncheon."

"Um, okay. Thanks . . ." Carly pushed open the door and dragged her suitcase into the next room. It was full of cute chairs and little side tables and landscape paintings.

This must be the sitting room. She rolled the suitcase through the next door, into a spacious bedroom with a huge canopied bed and French windows that opened onto a balcony.

Well, Carly thought, *I'm here. I made it.*

It was the same thought she'd had when she'd seen Mortmain Castle from the plane a few minutes ago. Somehow it didn't feel as triumphant now. It was an overwhelmed, exhausted little thought.

She flopped down on the bed and pulled her phone out of her jeans pocket.

Carly found herself praying that the messenger app would work. She really needed to hear her parents' voices right now . . .

"Honey, is that you?" Her mom's voice was groggy. Carly realized that with the time difference, it was the middle of the night in Ohio.

"Oh, Mom, sorry if I woke you!"

"Don't be silly! I was trying to wait up until I heard from you. Did you make it there okay?"

"Yeah, I'm at Mortmain Castle now."

"It's so good to hear from you! Let me put you on speaker. How was the flight?"

"Long, but really comfortable. And I have a bodyguard."

Sal's voice came over the line. "Nice! I wonder how much he costs. Maybe we can hire him for your prom."

"Ew, Sal! I'm gone for one day and you turn into Gross-Macho-Man Dad on me?"

"Just kidding. So how's the castle? You settling in?"

"Um, yeah. I mean, I'm sure I will once I've been here more than five minutes."

Her mom's voice chimed in again. "Just be careful, honey. You don't have to do anything that you're not comfortable with."

Carly thought of the way she'd been shuffled around in the past few hours. The way she'd been instructed to get in vehicles and follow people around and let other people carry her stuff. But that was all so small. Obviously her mom was talking about bigger things—the kinds of things she worried about whenever Carly went to a party or spent the night with friends.

"Okay. I'd better go now. I'll check in with you later. Love you!"

After the call ended, Carly looked around at her enormous, glittering new bedroom.

She was Charlotte Valmont, Princess Royal of the Kingdom of Evonia.

She was second in line for the throne.

And she had never felt so small.

5

Carly hadn't planned to fall asleep. She knew
her best chance of fending off jet lag was
to stay awake all day, even though she felt
completely fried.

But an hour and a half after she called her
parents, Seton's knock on the door jolted her
out of a doze.

"Ten minutes to noon, your highness."
His clipped, slightly bored voice was already
starting to become familiar.

Carly sat up groggily. Her new bed was
unreasonably soft. She'd blame the bed for
making her fall asleep. "Be right out!"

She scrambled to change into something
"business casual." She had packed all her best

clothes for this trip, but they all looked shabby when she held them up to the ornate floor-length mirror.

Finally she settled on a cute sundress, ran a brush through her hair, splashed some water on her face, and—

"Your highness? Two minutes to noon."

"Coming!"

They were five minutes late to lunch. That was how long it took to walk from Carly's set of rooms to the dining room. Lord G and Arthur sat at a table that was big enough to fit ten people. Arthur was already digging in, though Lord G had made a point of waiting for her.

"Look who decided to show up," said Arthur, shooting her an unfriendly look.

"Sorry—" Carly started, but Lord G cut her off.

"Never mind, my dear. As long as your food isn't cold yet, no harm done." Lord G pointed to the chair across from Arthur. Carly sat down. She looked over her shoulder to thank Seton for taking her here, but he had already left the room.

"Queen Emilia wanted me to tell you that she's sorry she can't be here to meet you today," Lord G told her. "She's had a cold all week and wasn't feeling up to leaving the royal palace. But she hopes you can visit her there soon."

"Ooo, what a treat," muttered Arthur. "The old bat never wants to see *me*."

"She sees you all the time, Arthur," said Lord G. Carly thought he sounded slightly defensive. "Every major holiday, not to mention every wedding and funeral and christening in this family—"

"Yes, of course, how could I forget those photo ops?" Arthur shot back. "So much quality time together, shuffling into place and waiting for the photographer to take eighty shots. Truly heartwarming. I'd guess the last time I had a private conversation with Queen Emilia was at *my* christening."

Carly couldn't decide whether to dislike her cousin or feel sorry for him. Queen Emilia didn't exactly sound like a warm-fuzzy type of grandparent figure. Not that Lord G was either. If Arthur's dad was dead and his mom had given up on him, that didn't leave him with many options for family bonding.

Then again, if he treated everyone the way he'd treated *her* so far, she could understand why people kept their distance from him.

Lord G turned back to her. "The fact is that you, Charlotte, are second in line for the throne. The queen is anxious to see you for herself and judge how ready you are for the responsibility."

This caught Carly off guard. "Um—how ready do I need to be at this point?"

Lord G dabbed at his mouth with a finely embroidered napkin. "Queen Emilia is ninety-two years old. Her son, Crown Prince Humphrey, is seventy—and in rather poor health. To be blunt, my dear, I am afraid you can expect to become queen sooner rather than later."

"Oh." This was more intense than she'd expected.

For weeks, she'd been thinking *I'm going to be a queen!* But that thought had always ended in *someday*. Not *literally any day now*.

"When you graduate from your American high school next year, the queen would like you to move to Evonia permanently."

Carly felt as if someone had punctured her lungs like balloons, letting all the air drain out of them. Next year was so soon—so sudden.

Leaving her family and friends for two months was one thing. Moving thousands of miles away from them for the rest of her life was totally different. And what about college? She'd been thrilled that she didn't *need* to go, but she'd still expected to apply. Her mom and Sal always talked about the great experiences they'd had at college. The friends they'd made. The adventures they'd had. The ways their world had expanded. Carly felt her own world shrinking to the size of a tiny dot on the map of Europe.

Of course it made sense. She'd figured she would eventually move to Evonia, but she'd thought it wouldn't be until she actually became queen. And she'd been imagining herself taking on that role at some point in her thirties.

Or maybe she hadn't really imagined it happening at all. Not for real. The whole thing had been a vague fantasy in her head, a sparkly excuse to not worry about anything or plan for her future.

Carly hoped she didn't look as stricken as she felt. If she did, Lord G didn't seem to notice. "In the meantime," he went on, "Queen Emilia wants me to begin teaching you about your royal duties."

"If you're up to it," snickered Arthur.

Carly froze with her fork halfway to her mouth. Slowly she set it down and looked over at her cousin. "What's that supposed to mean?"

Arthur shrugged. "It's a demanding job, being an heir to the throne. A delicate little thing like you might not be cut out for it."

Delicate little thing? Carly gripped her fork so hard that she half-expected it to snap. "I appreciate your concern," she said coldly. "But since you don't actually know me, I'm not sure you're the best judge of what I'm cut out for."

She turned to Lord G, straightening up in her chair. "I look forward to learning more about my responsibilities as an heir to the throne."

Her grandfather smiled at her. "Excellent. We'll start first thing tomorrow."

6

"First thing tomorrow" turned out to be six in the morning. Carly stumbled out of bed, still half-asleep, to join Lord G for breakfast. She was relieved to find that Arthur wasn't there.

"Right," said Lord G briskly as soon as she sat down at the table. "Here's your copy of today's schedule."

He slid a crisp piece of paper across the table. Carly picked it up and scanned the agenda on it.

6:30 a.m. - drive to Alaborn

7:00 a.m. - shopping with Lady Corinne

10:00 a.m. - meet Crown Prince Humphrey

11:00 a.m. - meet LePointe family

Noon - luncheon with communications minister and his family

1:00 p.m. - meet Overton family

2:00 p.m. - visit royal chapel and cemetery (P)

3:00 p.m. - meet tourism minister

4:00p.m. - tea with Prime Minister Clement

And so on, until 8:00 p.m.

"Three hours for shopping?" was the first question Carly asked.

"Trust me, my dear, you need it."

Since she was still barely awake, Carly let that dig slide. "Isn't Lady Corinne Arthur's mother?"

"Yes. And a member of one of Evonia's greatest noble families, the Irvines."

"If she doesn't have time for Arthur, why does she have three hours to take me shopping?"

"Because you are Princess Charlotte Frederika Isabelle Valmont."

Carly suppressed a frustrated sigh. That didn't seem like a fair answer. And this didn't seem like the ideal way to learn about her new country or her future duties. "Could we maybe go to the national museum at some point? I noticed that it's really highly rated on most tourism websites . . ."

Lord G gave her a stern look. "There is nothing you can learn in a museum that you can't learn from me."

"Oh . . . kay." Carly looked back down at the schedule. "What's this *p* in parentheses at two o'clock?"

"Short for 'photographers.' There'll be a few at the cemetery."

"What? Why?"

"Because it's good publicity, my dear. *You* are good publicity. Our people love you."

"But I've never been here before," said Carly, confused. "They don't know anything about me."

Lord G smiled. "Which is why you'll

be so easy for them to love. You're about to become the country's biggest celebrity. Shall we get going?"

***

The twenty-minute drive to the capital city was a longer version of yesterday's car ride: Carly and Lord G in the backseat, Seton and the driver up front. Carly was grateful that Arthur wasn't tagging along. This was stressful enough as it was.

Photographers. Celebrity. Our people love you. Her mind kept looping back to that. Maybe she shouldn't be surprised that a future queen would be famous in her own country. But it felt creepy. Was her picture going to end up on Evonian news sites? In Evonian tabloids?

"Now then," said Lord G as the car sped down the single country road that led away from the estate. "Think of me as your museum. What questions do you have for me?"

Carly tried to put the photo op out of her mind. She looked down at the schedule.

43

"Well, for starters, can you tell me more about these families? The LePointes, the Overtons . . ."

"Oh dear." Lord G sighed. "You're not familiar with the names of our noble families, are you?"

"Well," said Carly, a little defensively, "that's not the kind of thing that was covered in the guidebook. And I haven't had time to check every corner of the Internet for information about Evonian nobility."

Lord G grimaced. "The less you rely on the Internet, the better. I can see I'm going to have to start with the basics."

The basics took up the whole ride to Alaborn.

". . . The line of succession goes through the oldest child. Queen Emilia was the oldest of five children. Her younger brothers and their descendants are all members of the royal family but they're very far down in the line of succession. The queen's heir, as you know, is Crown Prince Humphrey. And since he has no children, his heir would've been his younger sister, Princess Isabelle—my wife. After she died, our son Frederick—your father—took her place in line. And then when Frederick died, you took his place."

It was weird to hear someone call her dad Frederick. Carly's mom had always called him Rick. In fact, Carly remembered doing an Internet search for his name once, back in elementary school. *Rick Valmont* hadn't turned up any helpful results. If they had, she would've found out about this royalty stuff a lot sooner.

"And who's after me?" Carly asked. "I mean, what happens if I don't have any kids, like Crown Prince Humphrey didn't?"

"Then," said Lord G grimly, "the crown would go to Isabelle's next-oldest descendant. Your cousin, Arthur."

Carly let that sink in. "I guess that explains why he dislikes me so much. I'm the only person standing between him and a three-hour shopping trip with his mom."

Lord G snorted in amusement. "You do have a way of cutting straight to the heart of things, don't you, Charlotte?"

"Um, thanks?"

"You'll want to be careful what you say around Lady Corinne, though. Honesty doesn't have much charm for her."

Carly straightened up a bit. "I know how to be careful about what I say, m'lord. I'm captain of the debate team at school." She instantly regretted saying *that*—as if one extracurricular activity made her qualified to be a queen.

"Well, being captain of the 'keep quiet and smile' team would've been better," said Lord G. "But we'll work with what we've got."

Carly tried to push down her annoyance. "If you don't mind my asking, m'lord, how come you're the one walking me through all this? I mean, no offense, but you're not even a member of the royal family. Not by birth, anyway."

Lord G smiled wryly. "Very true. But I married Isabelle when we were both very young. I spent years in the midst of royal traditions. And after I lost her . . ." He trailed off, and Carly saw his face twitch a bit, as if he was fighting to control it. Then he snapped out of it. "I had to steer Frederick through everything. Your great-uncle Humphrey couldn't be bothered. Humphrey can never be bothered. And the queen didn't have the time. She trusted me to guide Frederick. And despite how *that* turned out, she's trusting me to guide you now."

Carly wanted to ask what he meant by that. What had gone wrong with her dad? Other than the fact that he'd died so young, of course.

But by now they were entering the capital city. The downtown area was a beautiful cluster of stone and brick buildings packed close together along winding streets. Looking out the car window, Carly felt as if she'd been transported back in time. Or into some fairy-tale setting outside of time.

What am I doing here?

The panicky thought rose up out of nowhere. Carly squashed it down. *You're Princess Charlotte Frederika Isabelle Valmont,* she told herself firmly. *You belong here as much as anybody.*

But it was harder to believe than she would've liked.

***

Lady Corinne was beautiful, fashionable, and perfect. And Carly disliked everything about her.

She was as polite as her son was rude. But it was fake politeness. At least Arthur's unpleasant behavior seemed genuine.

She chattered pleasantly the whole time she was with Carly, never letting Carly get a word in. She shuffled Carly through a massively overpriced department store, selecting outfits for her to try on. She decided which clothes and jewelry and perfume to buy. "Charge it to the Count of Linland's account," she told the clerk breezily when they were finally done.

And she completely ignored Seton, who was with them every step of the way. For some reason this annoyed Carly the most.

By the end of the shopping excursion, Carly had ten bags of clothes she didn't need. And zero patience left.

Lord G was waiting for her in the car, reading a book. "Don't worry," he said without looking up. "Now that you've got Corinne out of the way, everyone else will be delightful by comparison."

"Easy for you to say, m'lord," Carly said dryly. "Are you just going to sit in the car and read the whole day?"

"No, I'll be with you on all the other stops. To make certain you don't embarrass me."

"I'm touched."

"You should be," said Lord G, finally closing his book. "Plenty of people would give anything to be able to embarrass themselves on a world stage."

Carly wasn't sure whether to be amused or unsettled by that comment. She ended up feeling both.

***

Prince Humphrey, her great-uncle, lived in a massive stone house. Lord G insisted it wasn't a castle or a palace, just a house. The crown prince was a quiet, awkward man, a little older than Lord G but much less fit. He looked as if he didn't move around much. Or smile much.

They sat in an elegant, airless room and ate scones. After Lord G made the introductions, the conversation limped along. The scones were dry, but Carly ate several just to have something to do in the long stretches of silence.

"Your house is beautiful," Carly told the prince.

"Thank you." Then nothing.

Next she tried, "This is my first time visiting Evonia. I know about all the big tourist draws, but I'd love suggestions for places to go that are off the beaten path. Do you have any recommendations?"

He frowned, thought for a moment, then said, "Not really."

Her last-ditch effort was, "That's an amazing portrait on the wall. Who is it?"

Prince Humphrey looked where she pointed. He squinted at the portrait as if he'd never seen it before. "Oh. That's Queen

Charlotte the First."

"Every royal and noble household has a portrait of her," Lord G added. "There's one at Mortmain Castle that I'll point out to you, my dear."

Carly felt a fresh spark of irritation. *So the one interesting thing in this room turns out to be totally unoriginal. Great.* "Well," she said. "This one really brings her to life."

Prince Humphrey shrugged. "I didn't choose it. The queen picked out all the furnishings for Valmont House years ago."

After the way Lady Corinne had handled the shopping, Carly couldn't say she was surprised. It seemed as if being directly in line for the throne didn't involve making many decisions for yourself.

She picked up a fourth scone.

***

Back in the car, Carly stared at the schedule and bit her lip.

"That went well," said Lord G cheerfully.

"Uh, did it?"

"Certainly. You said nothing inappropriate."

"That's your measure of success?"

Lord G shrugged. "Well, how did *you* think it went?"

Boring. Frustrating. "Prince Humphrey seems—"

"Useless? Yes."

"I was going to say sad."

Lord G squinted thoughtfully at her. "You know, I never considered that."

Carly suppressed a sigh. *What is WRONG with these people?*

And how can they expect me to become one of them?

7

At two o'clock that afternoon, Carly stood in front of her grandmother's grave. *Her Royal Highness, Princess Isabelle Emilia Alexandra Valmont* was engraved on the elaborate headstone. The grave next to it belonged to her uncle, Sir Walter Valmont. Visiting these graves was even stranger than the times her mom had taken her to visit her dad's grave back in Ohio. At least she'd occasionally thought about her dad, imagined what he was like. She had no frame of reference at all for this dead grandmother and uncle.

"Can I ask how Arthur's dad died?" Carly said to Lord G, who stood beside her. She pointed to Sir Walter's headstone.

"Car accident," said Lord G grimly. "Walter was a walking stereotype to the very end. Much like his son."

The words hit Carly like a bucketful of ice. *How can he talk about his own son that way?* "What does that mean?"

Something over by the cemetery gate caught Lord G's attention. "It means you'd better look serious and somewhat grief-stricken because the photographers are here."

Carly whipped her head around to follow his gaze.

"Don't look at them," Lord G said irritably. "That defeats the purpose. Just carry on as you were before. You were doing very well."

Carly glared at him. "I wasn't pretending."

"Even better. Carry on with that. It'll be good for the public to see you paying your respects."

It boggled Carly's mind that Lord G seemed so comfortable with the paparazzi intruding on this private moment. More than that: he'd *invited* them. And he seemed to think it was Carly's job to perform for them.

Carly stepped to one side so that Seton blocked her from the photographers' view.

"None of that," said Lord G. "Seton, give us some space."

"You're supposed to protect me," Carly hissed at Seton.

"Protect you from actual threats to your life," said Seton. "Not from your life itself, your highness."

Her bodyguard retreated to a spot about twenty feet away from them.

This is ridiculous, Carly fumed silently. *This whole day is ridiculous.*

And it wasn't even over yet.

***

The prime minister of Evonia smiled at Carly across yet another plate of scones. Carly felt like she had eaten at least thirty scones today. She picked up another one.

"How lovely that you're finally seeing Evonia," said Prime Minister Clement. "And are you in finishing school?"

"Am I—finishing school? Yeah, I'll be

starting my senior year in September—"

"No, dear," Lord G cut in. "Finishing school is a type of boarding school for young ladies. You're attending a public school in the United States, yes?"

"Oh. Yes. Not a boarding school, no. But it's a good school. I mean, my teachers say I have a good chance of getting into a top college."

The prime minister looked intrigued. "You plan to go to university? That's interesting. Most of the Valmonts don't. Do you know what you plan to study?"

The honest answer was no. She hadn't settled on anything, had been too torn by everyone else's different expectations for her. But when she opened her mouth, she realized a different answer was on the tip of her tongue. "I—well, I think I might major in something like international studies in undergrad. And then maybe go to law school after that."

"*Very* interesting," said the prime minister. "What sparked your interest in law?"

"I like researching things," said Carly, perking up. "And convincing people to agree with me."

The prime minister grinned. "A highly useful skill."

"Yeah. And . . ." She set her scone down, choosing her words. "I've always liked fixing things that aren't fair, or things that just don't make sense. For example, when I was twelve, my brother Rafe wanted a pet rabbit, but my mom and stepdad weren't on board with that. I came up with a list of reasons why it would be a good idea. Rafe would take care of the rabbit, so he'd learn to be more responsible. And we'd get it from an animal shelter—rescuing a rabbit that needed a home."

"Did it work?" the prime minister asked very seriously. Carly appreciated that he was actually listening to this slightly silly story.

She grinned. "It did. Rafe still has that rabbit." She saw Lord G raise his eyebrows at her. Clearing her throat, she added, "Anyway, that kind of educational background could be useful for me down the road."

"I suppose so," said the prime minister cautiously. "Though it would be more useful for someone with *my* job. Your career is going to be in public relations, really. Managing your image, your family's image."

The half-digested scones in Carly's stomach suddenly felt very heavy.

"Oh, but I'm not downplaying it," the prime minister assured her. "It's *very* important that royals know how to behave. And it's not as easy as it looks."

"Yeah," Carly sighed. "I've picked up on that."

***

The sun had set by the time they got back at Mortmain Castle. Carly had eaten so many scones that she'd barely touched her dinner. Being at a fancy restaurant with strangers— another noble family that was vaguely related to her—hadn't helped. She felt totally drained as she trudged inside with Lord G and Seton.

In the front hall, Lord G pointed to the portrait at the top of the staircase. "Queen

Charlotte the First. I like our painting better than the crown prince's, personally."

Carly crossed her arms and studied the portrait. Charlotte the First was middle-aged in this one, swimming in jewel-studded gown with puffy sleeves and a puffy neckline. She'd been younger in Prince Humphrey's portrait. Younger and less bored-looking. "Well, it's *bigger*."

Before Lord G could reply, Arthur's voice echoed across the hall. "Hail the conquering heir to the throne," he called from the top of the stairs.

Lord G let out a loud sigh. "I'm going for my nightly walk. Charlotte, Arthur, I'll see you both in the morning."

As soon as he was gone, Arthur came down the stairs, blocking Carly's path.

He held up his phone. "Looks as though you had a good day. If the media can be trusted. You're all over the gossip sites. I suppose you do look good from a distance."

Carly bit the inside of her mouth for a moment. Then she said calmly, "I think

I look just as good up close, not that it's anyone's business."

"Wrong on both fronts," said Arthur smugly. "First of all, up close it's clear that you're unpolished and ignorant. You don't know anything about Evonia. You don't have a clue how to be a princess. The charm of your outsider act is going to wear off fast."

Carly sucked in her breath—but clearly Arthur wasn't finished.

"And secondly, it's every Evonian citizen's business. You're going to represent them to the world someday. They own you, and you have to give them as much of yourself as they ask for. Pictures, interviews, parades where you stand on a balcony and wave. That's your job. You stay in your lane, or you get disgraced. And do you know what the Valmont family does with its disgraces? Erases them."

For a long moment, he just glared at Carly, silently daring her to come up with a retort. Which she couldn't. *Bet he spent all day working on that speech*, she thought furiously.

He sauntered past Carly, leaving the stairway clear.

***

Alone in her bedroom, Carly got out her phone and messaged her family. *Miss you all. How are you doing?*

But it was still Monday morning back in the States, so she didn't expect to hear back right away. Her parents would be at work. Her brothers would be sleeping late.

She pulled up a web browser on her phone and typed *Charlotte Valmont Evonia* into the search engine.

A picture of her cemetery visit popped up immediately, under the headline EVONIAN PRINCESS PAYS RESPECTS AT GRANDMOTHER'S GRAVE. Carly clicked on the brief write-up and scanned the comments.

I'm from Evonia originally and this warms my heart!

What a lovely girl—looks like Princess Isabelle!

She looks like a true princess!

Can't wait for this poised young lady to become queen. She'll put Evonia back on the map.

Lord G had gotten what he wanted: good publicity. And Carly felt vaguely gross. It was so weird that people who knew nothing about her were weighing in about everything from her appearance to her future.

She thought for a moment and then typed *Arthur Valmont* into the search engine.

Headlines from European news sites filled the results page.

ARTHUR VALMONT PUNCHES WAITER AT RESTAURANT

PRINCESS ISABELLE'S OUT-OF-CONTROL GRANDSON

ARTHUR VALMONT SETS FIRE TO BOARDING SCHOOL ATHLETIC FIELD

EVONIAN QUEEN'S GREAT-GRANDSON CRASHES CAR . . . AGAIN

"ARTHUR VALMONT TRASHED HIS HOTEL ROOM AND I HAD TO CLEAN IT": A MAID'S STORY

Well, no wonder everyone kept saying that it was important for royals to know how to behave. And no wonder Lord G wanted Carly to make the family look good.

Her phone buzzed. Rafe had just sent her a message. *Hey sis! Does Evonia RULE? Get it? Sorry, I'm still mostly asleep. Not at the top of my joke game.*

Out of nowhere, tears pricked at Carly's eyes. She wanted to be home in Ohio. She wanted to talk to her mom and Sal and kid around with her brothers and eat ice cream from Frozen Paradise instead of a thousand bad scones.

She didn't want to have to hold all of this Evonian drama in her brain and try to figure out how to feel about it. How to be okay with it.

But it looked as if she would have to. As Arthur had said—it was her job. Just like it had once been her dad's job. If her dad had handled it, she could too.

I'll show Arthur, she thought fiercely. *I'll prove that I can do this. I'm not going to let him scare me away.*

8

For the next two weeks, Carly paraded around Evonia meeting people. Or people visited her at Mortmain Castle. All the names and faces blurred together after a while. Several times, Carly noticed photographers zeroing in on her from a distance. And ordinary people with cell phones started showing up in the vicinity of Lord G's car. Seton made sure they didn't get "too close." Though Carly was starting to feel like everything and everyone was too close. The country was too small, the city was too crowded, even the Mortmain estate wasn't big enough for Seton to lose track of her.

Between social calls, Lord G had her take horseback riding lessons, tennis lessons, and etiquette lessons. The instructors he brought in to teach her these skills were as stiff and formal as the portraits in the front hall. They were always saying "Well done, your highness," in a tone that clearly meant the opposite.

In her rare hours of downtime, Carly had to study the family tree, memorize nobles' names and titles, practice proper table manners, and work on formal handshakes and waves. It was so mind-numbing that she started raiding Lord G's library for books on Evonian history. At night she'd immerse herself in the dramas of long-ago wars and power couples and trade agreements. Compared to everything else she had to learn, it was fascinating.

After dinner one night—her second Saturday in Evonia—she said to Seton, "I'd like to go for a walk. Is that cool with you?"

"I go where you go, your highness," he said. Which wasn't *No*, so Carly headed outside.

"How about an ice cream run?" she asked, pushing her luck. "I hear there's a great place in Alaborn."

He gave her a withering look. "I suggest we stay on the castle grounds."

Carly shrugged. "Worth a try."

So they wandered around the estate as the sun started to go down. Past the tennis court, past the stables, past the fancy gardens, past the maze made out of carefully trimmed bushes . . .

"Hang on. What's that little shed over there?" The white-painted wooden structure was so simple compared to everything else on the estate. It looked out of place.

"I'm not certain, your highness," Seton admitted.

"Let's check it out. Unless you think there are assassins lurking in there. Or paparazzi, for that matter."

Seton gave her blank look.

Right, no sense of humor, Carly remembered. "Come on."

The door to the shed was unlocked. Inside, Carly could make out some familiar shapes. A rocking horse. A sled. Two bicycles. Cardboard boxes were stacked on the floor. Carly leaned down to get a look at the labels on the boxes.

Frederick—old toys
Walter—photographs
Frederick—school essays (only his best)
Walter—rock collection

A model spaceship perched on top of one box. Carly carefully picked it up. It looked as if it had been built from a kit but put together slightly wrong. Some of the parts stuck out at wonky angles. "Whoa," Carly breathed. "This is all their old stuff. My dad's and uncle's stuff, from when they were kids. Normal kid stuff."

"Normal might be going too far," said Seton. "That ship is named the Duke of Space, according to the label on its wing."

Carly squinted, and sure enough, someone had written that name in awkward block letters. "How could you even see that from over there?" Carly asked Seton, astonished.

"Bodyguards have excellent vision, your highness. And we keep excellent track of time. It's nearly sundown. You should get back inside soon."

Reluctantly, Carly put the spaceship back down, closed the shed's door, and headed back the way she'd come. Seeing her dad's old stuff left a warm, pleasant feeling in her stomach. Not just the fact that the stuff had belonged to her dad—but the fact that someone had saved all of it. Someone had cared, had known it mattered.

"It really is beautiful here," Carly remarked to Seton. She pictured her dad and Arthur's dad racing around the estate on their bikes, or piloting The Duke of Space through the garden maze. "But I can't imagine what it would've been like to grow up in a place like this. It's so big and full of luxury, but at the same time it's, like, stifling, you know?"

"I have no comment," said Seton.

Which Carly figured meant Yes.

***

Back in her bedroom that night, Carly called her family. She didn't have many chances to catch up with her parents and brothers. The time difference made it especially hard. When she did talk to them, she always felt as if she might cry at any moment. Which she hated.

She also hated complaining. So when her family at home asked what she thought of her Evonian family, she didn't know what to tell them. She didn't *dislike* her grandfather. Lord G seemed to be doing his best, from his point of view. He hadn't been unkind to her. And she often found his wry comments amusing. But he also seemed to be purposely insensitive about things that should matter to him. Like whether his relatives—his own grandchildren—were happy.

Seton was actually all right. But Carly wasn't sure how to explain what she liked about him. Maybe it was the fact that she could tell him whatever she was thinking, even if he wouldn't respond. And that he beat her mercilessly every time she tried to play tennis with him. And that he'd gone on that walk with her tonight, no questions asked. But nobody who wasn't living here would understand why any of that mattered so much.

Then there was Arthur. He had kept a low profile after their talk on Monday night. But she still saw him at meals. Apparently he wasn't enough of a rebel to turn down Mortmain Castle's first-rate food. And he still hadn't said a single pleasant word to her. Best-case scenario, they ignored each other.

But she didn't tell her parents and brothers any of this. She stuck to vague, neutral comments, or tidbits that she could spin to be entertaining. Like she did tonight. "So I've been reading about Queen Charlotte the First. Did you know she was the first reigning queen of Evonia?"

"What does that mean?" asked Nic, his voice fuzzy through the phone.

"It means she ruled in her own right. She wasn't just married to the king. She was the one who decided that anyone born into the Valmont family would take the last name of Valmont, even if it came from their mother and not their father. Because she saw women as equal members of the family, equally important to carrying on the Valmont legacy. Isn't that cool?"

"Um, sure . . . if you think so," said Rafe.

Carly laughed. "Well we have the same name so I like learning about her. Plus, every royal and noble household in Evonia has a portrait of her. It doesn't have to be the *same* portrait, as long as there's a portrait. It's like an unwritten rule."

"Like most rules for Evonian royalty," her mom replied dryly. Which made Carly wonder how much her mom already knew about this experience. Maybe she understood more than Carly had thought.

She wanted to mention the shed with her dad's childhood stuff. But she was afraid it would make her cry for real. And she didn't want to bring it up in front of Sal, as if a guy she'd never known meant more to her than Sal did.

But after they hung up, Carly did something she'd never tried before. She looked up her mother online.

The most-viewed headlines were twenty years old.

HEIR TO THE EVONIAN THRONE MARRIES AN AMERICAN COMMONER

SCANDAL IN THE EVONIAN ROYAL FAMILY

**RUMORS SWIRL AROUND SECRET
ROYAL WEDDING**

**QUEEN EMILIA REFUSES TO MEET
GRANDSON'S NEW WIFE?!**

And then it got worse.

EVONIAN PRINCE DIES OF HEART ATTACK

**FREDERICK VALMONT: KILLED BY
A BROKEN HEART?**

**AN EVONIAN EMBARRASSMENT—
AN EVONIAN TRAGEDY**

Carly felt sick to her stomach. She shut her laptop a little too forcefully, then got up and walked to the window.

No wonder her mom had seemed so uneasy about Carly coming here. No wonder she hadn't been excited that Carly was in line for the throne. This was what happened to you when you were next in line. You got followed, gossiped about, lied about. Your life didn't belong to you anymore.

Arthur had been right about that.

9

"Good news," said Lord G at breakfast a week
later. "Queen Emilia is feeling well enough
to meet you. We'll go to the royal palace
tomorrow for an official introduction."

Arthur, sitting across from Carly, muttered
"Joy to the world" through a mouthful
of oatmeal.

Carly stuffed some food into her own
mouth so she wouldn't be able to snap back
at him. Besides, she felt kind of the same way
about meeting the queen.

"But first, here's today's schedule." Lord
G passed Carly the latest printout. Carly
instinctively scanned the page for a *(P)*.
There was always at least one. This time it

was at the very end of the agenda: *Visit Devoir Soup Kitchen*.

Carly held back a sigh. She ought to be used to putting on an act by now, but it just kept getting harder.

***

The soup kitchen was a surprisingly cheerful building. Kids' artwork hung on the walls, and large potted plants stood in the corners of the dining hall.

The people looked less cheerful. Some were lined up at the serving station to collect their food. Others were already sitting down at benches on the long tables. They all stared at Carly when she came in with Lord G and Seton. And they looked nothing like the fans who'd tried to get a glimpse of her. They looked bored, and maybe a little resentful.

The photographers were positioned near the entrance. They started snapping shots of Carly as soon as she walked in.

Lord G had explained the deal. The two of them were supposed to help serve meals for an hour. The soup kitchen's director bustled over to greet them, and moments later Carly was wearing a hairnet and gloves. She and Lord G joined an assembly line of servers. A staff member passed Lord G a bowl of soup. He put it on a tray, added a slice of bread, and passed it to Carly. Carly added a cup of fruit and handed the tray to the next person in line. Repeat, repeat, repeat.

It was an easy job, but Carly kept fumbling. The photographers' presence was distracting. And the people she was serving looked so unhappy with the whole setup. Carly was amazed that there was so many of them. She hadn't seen anyone panhandling on the streets. She'd only seen rich people in their fancy houses, fancy restaurants, fancy stores. Rich people and tourists. And now here were all these people with worn clothes and rough, wrinkled hands. All these people who clearly knew who she was and couldn't find the energy to care.

And why should they, really?

The next person in line was a boy about

Nic's age. Carly instinctively smiled at him. He looked surprised but smiled back. "Are you a melon fan or a grape fan?" Carly asked him, holding up two fruit cups. "Option number one has mostly melon. Option number two has more grapes."

"Uh . . ." The kid hesitated, then pointed to the cup with more grapes.

"Good choice. Grapes are, like, nature's candy, right?"

The kid snorted in amusement.

"Well done," murmured Lord G. "I hope the photographers caught that."

For a moment Carly wanted to throw a bowl of soup in his face and see if the photographers caught *that*.

But she could tell that just by being here, she was being disruptive. She didn't want to make it worse. This place was clearly doing good, necessary work. And these people deserved to get their food without Carly making it all about her.

***

In the car on the way home, Carly blurted out, "How can there be so many poor people in a country this small? Everything I've read makes it sound like your economy is pretty strong, thanks to all the tourism."

"Well, I'm not terribly familiar with the ins and outs of the tax code," said Lord G dismissively. "But my friends in other parts of Europe tell me it's a disgrace."

Carly frowned at him. "So—people like you are super rich, and ordinary people are super poor?"

"That's roughly it, yes."

His breezy tone was starting to get to her. "Can't somebody do something to fix that?"

"Somebody could, I suppose. Perhaps you can call up your friend the prime minister and ask him to look into it."

"You don't have to be sarcastic."

"My dear, I'm not being sarcastic. If you're concerned about something, you have a right, as an Evonian citizen, to take that concern to your government. Just don't expect *me* to have any say in the matter. Parliament makes the laws."

"You just benefit from them."

Lord G shrugged. "It's better than having us make the decisions. Believe me. Some of the older Valmonts like to ramble about the days when they had real power, and it makes me shudder. Really, it's much wiser to leave that to people who actually know what they're doing."

Carly had to admit that was a fair point. "But what if a member of the royal family *does* know what they're doing? What if somebody really cares about an issue and really understands it and—"

"Then you can start a charity foundation," said Lord G. "Or create an ad campaign. Your grandmother sponsored billboards that warned of the dangers of smoking."

Carly gaped at him. "I mean, that's great, but it's not the same as passing a law."

"No," Lord G agreed, speaking very deliberately. "That's the tradeoff we've made. We have our status for life—no need to run for election, no fear of being booted out. And in exchange, we don't try to run the country."

She remembered her brothers joking about how she would have to get the parliament's permission to open ice cream shops in Evonia. Suddenly she missed them and Sal and her mom so much it was physically painful.

How would she ever get used to living an ocean away from them? No matter how often they visited her here, it would never be the same. It wouldn't be home.

And without them around, nobody in Evonia would know the real Carly. Maybe the real Carly—the Carly who had opinions and went after concrete goals—would cease to exist. Instead she'd just be a nicely dressed girl going through the motions, smiling for the cameras.

Carly bit her lip, struggling to rein in her frustration. "I wish there hadn't been so many photographers."

Lord G shot her a truly puzzled look. "Oh? Why?"

"It just feels really dishonest. Like the whole thing was staged for their benefit."

"A little good PR never hurt anyone, Charlotte. I know you Americans have a saying about *any* publicity being good publicity, but in Evonia we see things differently."

Carly's throat stung. "So did we go there just for the good publicity? Not because we actually care about those people?"

Lord G gave her a thoughtful look. "It isn't that we don't care, Charlotte. It's just that we show it differently."

Carly had a feeling he wasn't talking about the soup kitchen at all. And that he meant to make her feel better.

It didn't work.

10

Arthur was waiting for her at the top of
the staircase, sitting beneath the portrait of
Charlotte the First.

"What's the matter? Had a bad day?"

Carly glared at him. "Arthur, I am not in
the mood."

"It's stressful, isn't it? Draining. All those
people watching you, demanding that you put
on a good show. You don't like putting on a
show, do you, Charlotte? You prefer substance.
And you'll never find that here. Maybe you
should follow your father's example."

"What's that supposed to mean?"

Arthur raised his eyebrows dramatically.
"He renounced his claim to the throne. Gave

up his place in the line of succession. Because he didn't have what it takes to fill the role. And he knew it. He would've taken you out of the running too, if that had been allowed."

"That's a lie!" The words came out as a shout. She couldn't force herself to sound calm and collected and mature anymore. "You're lying. I've researched the family history. I saw all the headlines about my dad marrying my mom, about them living in the States, about his death. I would've known if he'd given up his place in the line of succession."

Arthur let out a short, bitter laugh. "No, you wouldn't, because the press never knew. The public never knew. He did it right before he died. Literally turned in the paperwork and keeled over from the heart attack."

Carly clenched her fists. "Don't talk about that like it's a joke."

"Your father *was* a joke. He was pathetic. Weak. Just like you."

For the first time, Carly understood why someone would want to punch another person in the face.

It was so tempting. But she also knew in the back of her mind that this was what he wanted. To provoke her. To bring her down to his level.

So she didn't punch him.

But she did pin him against the wall so fast and so forcefully that she heard the breath wheeze out of him. His eyes got huge and round. His mouth opened and closed like a fish's.

"Don't. You. Ever. Insult *my* family. Again."

He managed a tiny nod. She let him go and backed off.

"Why do you keep baiting me?" she demanded. "Why do you want my life? Because I can't imagine why you would, if you think it's so smothering and miserable."

Arthur's face twisted. "I'd be better at it than you. My father would've been a wonderful king, if he'd had a chance. If he hadn't been the younger son. Or if your father had died before *you* were born, my father would've been Frederick's heir instead of you. He deserved it. He deserved to be king. Everything would've been different." He drew in a breath, steadying

83

himself. "And if people actually had to take me seriously, I'd be the best king this country's ever seen!"

Carly felt the sharpest edges of her anger fade. She could almost pity her cousin. He so obviously felt cheated out of something important—and he had been. He was just wrong about what it was. "Maybe if you tried being a decent *person* first, people would *choose* to take you seriously. Ever thought about that?"

She turned and left without waiting for him to respond.

***

Seton caught up to her as she charged down the hallway. He'd been right behind her on the stairs, like always. He must've seen the whole thing happen.

"Good thing you're not Arthur's bodyguard, huh?" she said to him through clenched teeth.

"A very good thing, your highness," Seton responded quietly.

Carly reached the door that led to her rooms. "I'm gonna be in here for a while, okay?" she said as she opened the door. "Can you tell my grandfather that I'm not feeling well and I can't make it to dinner?"

"I'll tell him, your highness. And I'll be waiting out here in case you change your mind."

"Thanks." Carly closed the door in his face. Then she called her mom.

"Hey, sweetie! How are—"

"Why didn't you tell me about my dad?" Carly's voice was ragged. She was finally crying, after weeks of wanting to. "Why didn't you tell me that he gave up his place in the line of succession?"

"I—Oh, honey. Who told you about that?"

"It doesn't matter who told me! *You* should've told me! You should've told me he wasn't actually a prince, he *chose* not to be a prince, and I don't have to be a princess!"

"Carly, what's going on? I thought you were excited for this opportunity. That's why I didn't object to you going over there. What's changed?"

"Everything!" Carly hated how melodramatic she sounded, but she couldn't help it. She'd been holding everything in for too long. "I thought I was following in my dad's footsteps. I thought he'd be proud of me for doing this. But he didn't want this! For himself or for me! And neither do I!"

Before her mom could respond, she ended the call and flung her phone onto her bed.

***

It wasn't actually that hard to give Seton the slip. First Carly changed into jeans and a T-shirt and grabbed her wallet. Then all she had to do was turn on some music at full blast, climb down the trellis beside her balcony, and walk through the estate's front gate.

As she set off on the road to town, she actually wished it was farther away. She wished she could keep walking forever.

11

The ice cream shop in Alaborn was tucked into a narrow alley. Only a simple wooden sign hung over the door. *Café Glace, Est. 1782*. Inside, the place was full of tourists, but none of them seemed to recognize Carly. It was easier to blend in without a bodyguard, a dignified grandfather, and a car with a chauffeur.

As she stood in line to order, her phone buzzed. Her mom was trying to call her on the messenger app. Carly turned her phone off.

Once she had her ice cream, she went outside and stood in the alley, away from the crowds of people. She didn't feel any better.

She felt like a child—like a coward. But at least the ice cream was good.

It took another half hour for Seton to track her down. When she saw him walk into the alley, she sighed.

"Are you here to kidnap me?"

"In a sense," said Seton. He glanced up at the sign above the shop door. "But first, what flavor do you recommend?"

"I just had the chocolate. It's really good, but I don't know what flavors you're into. You seem like more of a vanilla guy."

Seton shrugged. "I don't often indulge in ice cream."

"Shocking." Carly joined him in line. "I haven't gotten you in trouble with my grandfather, have I?"

"Me? No. Yourself, yes."

"Yeah, I'm okay with that. At least I haven't set anything on fire."

"As far as I know," Seton said sarcastically.

Carly snorted slightly. Even if everything about this day was miserable, at least she'd heard Seton crack a joke. Then she thought of her cousin and his rampages again. "You know, I kind of feel sorry for Arthur, up to a point. His dad died . . ."

"So did yours."

"Yeah, but I was too little to know what had happened. Too little to remember him. And I have an awesome stepdad. Not to mention an awesome mom. It doesn't seem like Lady Corinne is very close to Arthur. And he doesn't have siblings either. So in a way, he's really alone."

"As you know, he has a *large* extended family."

"Yeah, and as *you* know, they don't act like a family most of the time." Carly shrugged. "I'm not saying it's an excuse for the way he treats other people. I'm just saying, I wouldn't switch places with him. Or at least—I wouldn't switch *lives* with him."

"Good," said Seton. "Because I'm supposed to get you back to Mortmain Castle by sundown."

Two minutes later they were in Lord G's car. Seton sat in the back with Carly instead of up front with the driver. Carly smiled slightly as she watched him nibble at his scoop of ice cream.

She felt a knot of dread in her stomach at the thought of facing her grandfather. But she knew she needed to patch things up—and not just with him.

"Still glad you're my bodyguard instead of Arthur's?" Carly asked Seton.

"Extremely glad," said Seton, taking another lick of his ice cream.

***

Lord G was off on his nightly walk. Arthur was nowhere in sight either, to Carly's relief. Carly went to her room and called her mom back.

"Oh, thank goodness! I've been trying to reach you for ages. I want to help, honey. I'm here to listen. Talk to me, okay?"

Carly took a deep breath. "I'm sorry I yelled at you earlier. I was just really shocked."

"Honestly, Carly, there were times when I wanted to tell you everything. About your dad's decision, about the Valmonts, about why we drifted so far away from them. But you never really even asked about your dad. And I didn't want to overload you with stuff you weren't ready to hear."

"I get that," Carly said. "And I know I didn't ask you about my dad much. I wanted to. But I have Sal, and he's a great dad. I didn't want either of you to feel like something was missing from my life. Now, though—my dad's the only person who could've really understood what this is like. I just really wish I knew more about him. I wish he was here and I could just ask him what he thinks I should do."

Her mom let out a shuddering breath on the other end of the line. Carly realized she was probably crying. That made her feel awful—but also less alone.

"It's true that your dad didn't want to be a king," her mom said. "And he didn't want you to grow up with the same pressures and restrictions that he faced. But he also knew he couldn't renounce your rights *for* you. He couldn't make that decision on your behalf. He wanted you to make your own choice when you were old enough."

Carly found herself nodding, even though her mom couldn't see her. "Why didn't you warn me it was going to be so hard?" she asked in a small voice.

"Would you have believed me if I did?"

Carly let out a choked little laugh. "Probably not."

***

Carly had never figured out where Lord G went on his night walks. So she asked Seton where she could find her grandfather. And sure enough, he said "This way, your highness."

He led her to the little shed where her dad's and uncle's stuff was stored.

Lord G was inside, sitting on a stack of boxes, holding the battered toy spaceship. He didn't look up when Seton opened the door.

"Here she is, my lord," said Seton. "I'll wait out here." He nodded for Carly to step into the shed, then closed the door behind her.

Carly picked her way through the clutter and sat down next to Lord G. For a minute she couldn't think of anything to say. She didn't really think she owed him an apology. Finally she nodded at the spaceship. "Is that my dad's or Walter's?"

"I think it was originally Frederick's. But Walter always wanted everything Frederick had. And Frederick never wanted what we gave him. So I think he let Walter have this."

Carly nodded. "You're the one who saved all this stuff, aren't you?"

"Of course. What was I going to do, toss it out?"

"You don't seem like the most sentimental guy, you know."

"Oh, believe me, I know."

Carly asked a little timidly, "Does Arthur know about this shed?"

Lord G shrugged, still not looking at her. "I'm not sure. He might've stumbled upon it, like you did."

"I think he should know about it," Carly said. "I think you should talk to him about it.

And about his dad. And about—just stuff in general. It might help."

"You're giving out parenting advice now?" said Lord G with a touch of his usual dryness.

Carly shrugged. "Just an idea. It's harder to run away from people who seem human."

"Ah," sighed Lord G. "I suppose that's why you ran away?"

"I just needed some time to think straight. I wasn't running away. It's not like I could hide for long in a country the size of an airplane hangar anyway."

Lord G chuckled softly. "Fair point. And now that you've done your thinking, what are your thoughts?"

Carly took a deep breath. "I'll go to meet the queen tomorrow, like I'm supposed to. But I can't promise to make a good impression on her. I'm going to be honest and tell her that—that I don't know if I can do this. And if that makes her angry—if she thinks I'm weak and disappointing—I can live with that. I hope you can too. Even if it embarrasses you."

Lord G was quiet for a long moment, staring down at the little spaceship in his hands. Finally he cleared his throat. "My dear Charlotte, I admit I don't yet know you very well. But it's clear to me that you are an intelligent and thoughtful young woman. The exact opposite of your cousin. In short, you're exactly the kind of future monarch we need."

Carly sighed. "I appreciate that, m'lord. I just don't know if I'm—up to it."

Lord G nodded. "I had a similar conversation with your father sixteen years ago. I'll tell you what I told him. You may choose to leave the line of succession. But you will always be part of this family. I'm not like some of my wife's cousins, disowning children who don't toe the line. Perhaps because I'm not a Valmont. But like me, Carly, you're an Evonian citizen above all else. If you honor *that*, I personally will never be embarrassed by you."

It took Carly a moment to realize that for the first time, he'd called her by her nickname. "Thanks, Grandpa."

12

Lord G had been right about the palace. It really was even grander than Mortmain Castle. It was a long rectangular building made of white stone, with towering columns and seemingly endless windows. Inside, the reception hall was the length of a football field. Every surface Carly could see was black-and-white marble. Floor, ceiling, tapestry-covered walls.

"Seton and I will be right out here," Lord G told Carly.

"Wait, you're not coming in with me?" A bubble of panic swelled in her stomach.

Lord G smiled at her. "Queen Emilia wants to speak with you privately. And you'll do fine, my dear. I have no doubt of it."

Carly glanced from Lord G to Seton. Her bodyguard wore his usual unreadable expression. But he gave her a little nod. She took that as a sign of encouragement.

You can do this, Carly assured herself. *You're . . . you're Carly. You're just Carly and that's enough.*

***

Queen Emilia's private sitting room was all purple, which caught Carly by surprise. The queen herself was a tiny woman with papery skin and cotton-white hair. She sat in an armchair that actually looked somewhat comfortable.

Carly knelt down like she'd practiced with her manners tutor.

The queen waved a bony hand dismissively. "That's all right, child, get up. Have a seat on the sofa."

Carly moved over to the cushion-covered purple sofa. She knew she was supposed to let the queen lead the conversation. Her manners tutor had been very clear on that.

"You look very much like your grandmother," the queen remarked.

"I get that a lot," said Carly. Then she remembered that her grandmother was this woman's daughter. It must be so strange, so sad, to outlive your daughter *and* both your grandsons.

Queen Emilia studied her with beady eyes. "So what do you think of Evonia?"

Carly breathed in slowly, choosing her words. "There's a lot I like. And a lot that I can't stand."

The queen didn't blink. "Go on."

"I know you want me to live here after I graduate from high school. And I do want to learn more about Evonia. I want to feel like I belong here. But I don't want to just be a figurehead. I don't want to show up at parades and pose for photo ops. If I'm going to spend the rest of my life here, I want to do something that makes it feel worthwhile. I know that if I give up my place in the line of succession, Arthur will be king after Prince Humphrey. And I know everyone thinks that'll be a disaster." *Though maybe it wouldn't,* she thought. *Maybe if Arthur finally felt like he mattered, he'd shape up. Maybe he'd want to honor his dad's memory. And even if he was still a train wreck, at least he wouldn't have any actual power.*

Carly took another deep breath. Arthur's choices weren't up to her. She could only control her own decisions. "But I can't be the kind of queen this family wants. I can't live up to Charlotte the First."

"Ah yes," sighed Queen Emilia. "Well, who can live up to *her*? But between the two of us, I doubt your father named you after her. I think he named you after Charlotte Devoir, the eighteenth-century revolutionary. How much do you know about her?"

"Um—not much."

Queen Emilia raised her eyebrows.

"Not anything," Carly admitted quickly.

The queen nodded. "Well, I can recommend several good biographies of her. She was part of a rebel group in the late 1700s. She fought to bring down the monarchy and bring a more democratic government to Evonia."

"Whoooa," said Carly. "But—the monarchy didn't give up its governing powers until about fifty years ago, right?"

"Correct," said Queen Emilia. "The eighteenth-century uprising failed. But it inspired future generations. Charlotte Devoir believed that leaders should earn their power. And that everyone should have the freedom to pursue goals of their choosing. Regardless of their family or social class."

"The soup kitchen is named after her," Carly realized.

"Yes. And a wing in our largest hospital. And one of the parliament buildings."

Carly had a feeling she would've liked this lady.

"I suggest you follow Charlotte Devoir's example," Queen Emilia said. "Do not do what is expected of you. Do what you know you are suited to do—what you believe in."

Carly thought of the words she'd heard so often from her mom: "I want you to live the best life possible." Suddenly Carly realized she'd been misunderstanding those words. Her mom didn't want her to have a life that was comfortable and carefree. She wanted Carly to *live* a life she could be proud of.

"You know where your talents lie," said Queen Emilia. "You know what you can accomplish. Never mind those who say you must follow a certain path. Make your own path."

"Is that what you did?"

The queen smiled a little sadly. "No. And I regret it. But your father did. And so can you, my dear. There's no need for you to decide anything immediately. I'd lay odds that I have another decade in me. No promises on how long my son will last, but he certainly won't need a replacement tomorrow."

Carly smiled. "I'll keep that in mind."

***

For once, Arthur wasn't lurking around waiting to taunt her. Carly had to go looking for him.

She found him napping on one of the terraces. As she walked up to him, he opened his eyes and jumped to his feet. Carly thought he looked nervous. Her outburst last night must've rattled him. *Well, good*, she thought. *He was looking for a reaction, and he finally got one. Maybe now he'll start thinking twice before he lashes out at people.*

"Hi Arthur," Carly said calmly. "I just wanted to thank you for being so *blunt* with me about what it really means to be royalty. I understand a lot of things better than I did when I first got here."

Her cousin's expression turned smug again. "Oh, really? Well, glad to help."

"And I wanted to let you know that I'm going to officially give up my claim to the throne."

Arthur's smirk returned in full force. "I see. Well, it's for the best, really."

"Yeah, I think so," Carly agreed. "Because that way there won't be any conflict of interest when I run for parliament in about ten years."

The smirk didn't vanish right away. First it froze unnaturally, and then it twitched a bit, wavering. "Run for parliament?" Arthur repeated blankly.

Carly nodded, fighting to keep her own expression serious. "That's right. I figure, once I've got my law degree, I'll move back here and try to make a real difference. Who knows— maybe I'll be your prime minister someday."

That was when Arthur's grin crumbled, replaced by a look of pure horror.

Behind her, Carly could've sworn she heard Seton snort with laugher.

VANESSA ACTON is a writer and editor based in Minneapolis, Minnesota. She enjoys stalking dead people (also known as historical research), drinking too much tea, and taking long walks during her home state's annual three-week thaw.